BEVERLY CLEARY
JANET'S
Thingamajigs

ILLUSTRATED BY
DyAnne DiSalvo-Ryan

A Young Yearling Special

Published by
Dell Publishing
a division of
The Bantam Doubleday Dell Publishing Group, Inc.
666 Fifth Avenue
New York, New York 10103

ISBN: 0-440-40108-9

Reprinted by arrangement with William Morrow and Company, Inc.

Printed in the United States of America

November 1988

10 9 8 7 6 5 4 3 2 1

WAK

"I can't find the thingamajigs," Mother said when
Jimmy fell down and skinned his knee. "What
happened to the thingamajigs?"

Thingamajigs was a word Mother sometimes
used when she was excited or in a hurry. Janet,
who was Jimmy's twin sister, enjoyed finding out
what thingamajigs meant each time her mother
used the word. This time it meant Band-Aids.

While Mother took care of Jimmy's knee, Janet found a red plastic paper clip, a little wheel, and a shiny bead. They were just right to hold in her hand. "Are these thingamajigs?" she asked.

Mother laughed and said, "Yes, you could call those thingamajigs."

Janet carried her things around all morning. She showed them to Mr. Lemon, the mailman. "See my thingamajigs," she said.

"Well, what do you know? Thingamajigs!" Mr. Lemon sounded surprised.

At lunchtime, Janet laid her plastic paper clip, her little wheel, and her shiny bead on a chair in the living room and said, "I don't want Jimmy to touch these things."

"They're just old stuff," said Jimmy, who wanted very much to touch them, so he did. He touched them every time Janet wasn't looking. He liked to hold them, too.

He touched them until Janet caught him at it and said, "Jimmy, those are *my* thingamajigs."

"No," said Jimmy, holding on to them.

"Mother, Jimmy won't give me my thingamajigs," said Janet, "and I asked him in a nice, polite voice."

"I'm not hurting them," said Jimmy, who could be stubborn.

"Jimmy, give me my thingamajigs!" yelled Janet. Her voice was not polite at all.

"No," said Jimmy and turned his back.
Janet pushed Jimmy. Jimmy yelled, "Janet is pushing me!" Then he pushed Janet.

"Children!" cried Mother as she came out of the kitchen. "Stop this at once. Jimmy, give Janet her little things. You can find toys of your own."
Jimmy threw Janet's things on the floor. "I don't want other toys!" he shouted.

Janet picked up her things and put them back on
the chair. "I don't want Jimmy to touch my
thingamajigs," she said.

Mother said, "Janet, you cannot leave them on
that chair. When Daddy comes home, he wants to
sit on the chair. He doesn't want to sit on your
toys. If you don't want Jimmy to touch your
things, you should put them away."

So Janet found a paper bag in the kitchen. She put the red plastic paper clip, the little wheel, and the shiny bead into the bag, wrapped a rubber band around the top, and put it in her crib. "Now Jimmy can't touch my thingamajigs," she said.

"I don't want to touch Janet's things," said Jimmy, but he *did* want to touch them, more than anything.

The next day, Janet found a spool, a doll's shoe, and a smooth green stone. She carried her new little things around while Jimmy pretended to put air in the tires of his dump truck. She showed them to Mr. Lemon when he brought the mail. Then she laid her little things on a chair and went into Mother and Daddy's room to help Mother make the big bed. When she came back, Jimmy was not playing with his dump truck. He was holding her spool, her doll's shoe, and her smooth green stone.

"Jimmy is touching my thingamajigs!" Janet cried. "He took them from the blue chair!"

"Children, I am at my wit's end," said Mother.

"What does 'at my wit's end' mean?" asked Janet.

"It means I don't know what to do," answered Mother. "Jimmy, give Janet her things."

Jimmy threw the toys on the floor. "I am too big for those things," he said. "They're just junk."

"They are not junk," said Janet. "They are my treasures."

Jimmy only pretended to play with his dump
truck while she picked up her treasures and laid
them on the blue chair again.

"Janet," said Mother, "you cannot leave your
things on the blue chair. I do not want to sit on
your toys. I told you if you don't want Jimmy to
touch them, you should put them away."

"I am at my wit's end," said Janet. Then she found another paper bag in the kitchen. She put her spool, her doll's shoe, and her smooth green stone into her paper bag. She put a rubber band around the top of the bag and put it in her crib. "Now Jimmy can't touch my thingamajigs," she said.

The next day the same thing happened with a
feather, a piece of pink yarn, and an old lipstick
case. And the day after that the same thing
happened with a little stick, a pretty leaf, and an
empty snail shell. Every day Janet found little
things, and every day she put them into paper bags
in her crib, where Jimmy could not touch them.

One day Mother said, "Janet, your crib is full of paper bags. When you go to bed, you rustle like a mouse in a wastepaper basket. Don't you want to share some of your paper bags with Jimmy?"

"No," said Janet as she climbed over the rail of her crib. "These are my paper bags."

"Oh dear, what are we going to do?" asked Mother. "Janet's crib is so full of paper bags she rustles like a mouse in a wastepaper basket. There is scarcely room for her to sleep. What are we going to do?"

"Paper bags are silly," said Jimmy as he climbed over the rail of his crib. Neither twin would let Mother lower the side of a crib. Climbing over the rail was fun.

"Paper bags are not silly," said Janet. "Paper bags are nice."

"But, Janet, you have too many," said Mother. "We will have to find another place for all your paper bags."

"I like being a mouse in a wastepaper basket," said Janet, and she went right on finding little things and putting them in paper bags in her crib. Every night she said, "*Squeak-squeak.* I am a little mouse."

"*Grr-grr.* I am a fierce bear," said Jimmy. He did not sound like a fierce bear. He sounded like a cross boy.

Then one morning Mother said, "Today we are going to have a surprise."

"Is it strawberries?" asked Jimmy.

"Is it a nice soft kitten?" asked Janet.

"No, it isn't strawberries or a nice soft kitten," answered Mother. "You wait and see."

Jimmy and Janet thought and thought, but they could not think what Mother's surprise could be.

"If you watch out the front window, you will see it sometime this morning," said Mother.

Jimmy and Janet watched out the front window.
"When is it going to come? When is it going to
come?" they asked over and over. They saw a boy
riding a bicycle, a girl skipping rope, and a lady
carrying a shopping bag. They saw cars, a tow
truck, and a school bus, but they did not see a
surprise. After a while they grew tired of watching
and turned their little table upside down and
pretended it was a boat.

And then, when the twins happened to look out the window, a big delivery truck came slowly down the street, paused, and turned into the driveway—Jimmy and Janet's driveway. Two men got out of the truck. They opened the back, lifted something out, and set it on the grass. It was a bed.

They lifted out another bed and set it on the grass, too. Grown-up beds!

"Beds!" shouted Jimmy and Janet. "Mother, are these beds for us?"

"Yes," answered Mother. "You are growing up. It is time for you to have big beds."

The men carried one bed into the house and set
it on Janet's side of the bedroom. They carried the
other bed into the house and set it on Jimmy's side
of the room. "There you are, kids," one of them
said. "Sleep tight, and don't let the bedbugs bite."

Jimmy and Janet bounced up and down on their
new grown-up beds while Mother stood in the hall
and watched. Then Jimmy stopped bouncing.
"What is Janet going to do with her paper bags?"
he asked. "They will fall off her bed."

Janet stopped bouncing. She took her paper bags
from her crib and piled them on her new bed.
When she climbed back on her bed, paper bags slid
off all over the floor.

"Ha-ha," said Jimmy.

"Jimmy can have my old paper bags," said Janet.
"I am not a mouse. I am a big girl, and I sleep in a
big bed."

"I don't want Janet's paper bags," said Jimmy. "I am too big to play with little junk."

"So am I," said Janet.

The twins began to bounce again. "We are big! We are big!" they sang while Mother tried to gather up all of Janet's paper bags.

Then Jimmy and Janet heard Mr. Lemon poking letters and catalogs through the slot in the front door. They jumped off their beds and ran to meet him. "Mr. Lemon! Mr. Lemon!" they shouted when they opened the door. "We have big beds! We have big beds!"

"Wow! Big beds!" said Mr. Lemon.
Jimmy and Janet could tell he was really surprised.
"Say, you *are* growing up!" said Mr. Lemon. "I never would have guessed."

Growing up—that was what Jimmy and Janet
wanted more than anything in the whole world.
"We are growing up!" they shouted. "We are
growing up!"